PERRY POPPETT

by

LILLIAN CLARK

ILLUSTRATED
· BY
ANNE ALLABEN

John Martin's House, Inc.

KENOSHA, WISCONSIN

Perry Poppett
lived in a
little red
house.
He had red hair.
And he had—

A gay
red
see-saw,

A little red wagon,

A smooth
red swing.

He had—

A sparkling
red sand-box,
filled with
shining sand.

He had—

A bright red pail

and shovel.

And he had—

A beautiful new

RED BALL.

That's what he liked
best of all.

BOP!

He bounced it

HIGH

on the

sidewalk.

Bucky came over and begged,
"Let me bounce it!"

"No," Perry answered.

BOP! BOP!

Then Bucky GRABBED it!

Away he ran,

with the ball—

With Perry right
behind him.

He ran around

the see-saw, and—

He ran around

the wagon.

He ran around
the swing
and he

ran around the sand-box—

And
he ran around the pail.

He ran around

the shovel.

He ran around to
the lot around the corner,
where some big boys were
playing baseball.

Bucky threw
Perry's ball

back to him. "I want

to play on your team!"
he called to the big boys.

"I want to play too!"
Perry Poppett
called.

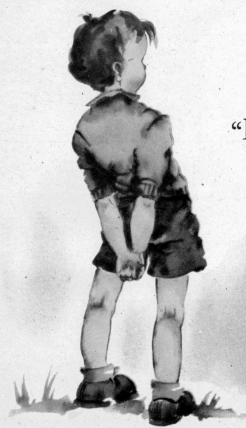

"No—Go home!" the
big boys shouted.
"You might get hurt!

You're both too little."

Perry and Bucky backed away.

Perry and Bucky slowly
turned and walked away.

S–L–O–W–L–Y

They walked back to

Perry's house.

BOP! BOP!

Perry bounced his ball again.

It was such a lively ball

that it bounced high

with just a TAP.

Bucky
watched.

Soon Perry cried, "CATCH!"

And twirled his arm around.

"This is better than bouncing,"
he shouted, and pitched to
Bucky.

Bucky caught it
and pitched
it back.

Pitch! and catch!
Pitch! and catch!
The gay new ball flew

fast between them.

"Now WE have a TEAM!"
Bucky shouted.